Grandpa Jack
and the
Legend of Santa's Helpers

by Chuck Karnehm

DORRANCE
PUBLISHING CO
EST. 1920
PITTSBURGH, PENNSYLVANIA 15238

Dorrance Publishing Co
585 Alpha Drive
Pittsburgh, PA 15238
Visit our website at *www.dorrancebookstore.com*

ISBN: 978-1-6491-3337-3
eISBN: 978-1-6491-3304-5

Grandpa Jack
and the
Legend of Santa's Helpers

It was a cold snowy day and Tommy was relieved that it was Friday; he couldn't wait to get home. Some of the boys in his second-grade class were making fun of him because he still believed in Santa Claus. Tommy loved everything Christmas and Santa Claus was very real to him.

"Only babies believe in Santa Claus," Billy jeered.

"Santa isn't real," Jimmy added.

"Hey Tommy," Nick yelled. "Ho Ho Ho, is Santa real? No No No!"

"Stop it you guys. Santa IS real!" Tommy yelled.

As Tommy was running out of school, he could hear the boys laughing at him.

When Tommy got home from school, he was in a bad mood.

"What's wrong Tommy?" his mother asked.

"The boys in my class were making fun of me; they said that Santa isn't real. I told them that Santa is real," said Tommy. "But they kept making fun of me. I never want to go back to school."

Tommy ran upstairs and slammed his bedroom door.

"Hmmm," thought Mom. She had an idea. She reached for her phone and made a call.

A few minutes later, there was a knock at the door. Tommy's mom smiled as she opened the door to find Grandpa Jack.

"Oh Dad, I'm glad you are here," said Katie. "Tommy is in his room; he is really upset because of what the boys were telling him at school today."

Katie filled Grandpa in on how the boys were teasing him about believing in Santa Claus.

"Dad, will you talk with Tommy? I know that you will know what to do," she said with a wink.

Grandpa Jack went up to Tommy's room. He was lying on his bed looking up at the ceiling and tears were running down his cheeks.

"Hey, Tommy, what are you doing?" asked Grandpa.

"Nothing Grandpa, just lying here thinking," sniffled Tommy.

"Heard you had some trouble in school today," said Grandpa.

"Yeah, some of the boys in my class were not very nice. They told me there was no such thing as Santa Claus and they made fun of me because I said there IS a Santa Claus," said Tommy.

"Do you want to take a ride with me?" asked Grandpa.

"Sure, where are we going?" Tommy asked.

"I have a few errands to run, and I think we should talk," said Grandpa.

They got into Grandpa Jack's car and drove across town. Grandpa Jack stopped his car in front of a house that Tommy hadn't seen before.

"Who lives here Grandpa?" asked Tommy.

"Well, your Great-Great-Grandpa Chuck used to live here," said Grandpa Jack. "And when I was a little boy, I used to come over here to see him."

"Is he in the house now?" asked Tommy.

Grandpa Jack laughed a little bit and said, "No, Tommy, Great-Great-Grandpa Chuck passed away a long time ago. The reason I brought you over here is to tell you a secret that he told me when I was in the second grade. It might help you with those boys at school."

Tommy turned to face Grandpa Jack with a questioning look on his face.

"You know, Tommy, when I was your age, the boys and girls were telling me the same thing about Santa not being real. I didn't believe them. I knew Santa was real. But they still made me mad, just like they made you mad today. I told my Grandpa about these kids in school that were making fun of me. He asked me if I would take a ride with him and told me he had a really big secret to share."

"WOW, Grandpa did he tell you the secret?" asked Tommy.

"Yes, he did, Tommy, and now I'm going to tell you, but only if you can promise not to tell anyone about this," said Grandpa.

"Yes, Grandpa, I promise," said Tommy.

"You really promise, Tommy? It's very important," Grandpa Jack said.

"I promise. Please tell me. PLEASE!" pleaded Tommy.

Grandpa Jack looked at the house and had a little smile on his face and a gleam in his eye as he recalled so many years ago the time he took a car ride with Grandpa Chuck.

He started, "Grandpa Chuck told me that he had tried to catch Santa putting out the presents every Christmas Eve. He fell asleep every year and vowed the next year to catch him. But when the next year came around, he fell asleep again! Then one Christmas Eve, when he was in second grade, he woke up and heard some noise in the living room near the Christmas tree. He slowly tiptoed out of his room, and sure enough, there was Santa putting the toys under the tree. Grandpa Chuck said that he couldn't believe his eyes, standing in front of HIS tree was SANTA CLAUS! He had finally seen him."

Tommy's eyes were as big as saucers as he listened in awe. "He really saw Santa Claus?" asked Tommy.

"Yep, and Santa turned around and even said, 'Hello' to him. Grandpa Chuck told Santa that he had been trying to catch him for years but always fell asleep. Santa told him he always knew what was going on and waited until he was sure he was asleep before he put the presents under the tree."

Grandpa Chuck asked Santa, "Why didn't you wait until I fell asleep this year?"

"Well, I let you catch me this year," Santa said. "We need to talk."

"Santa told Grandpa Chuck that he liked how he really believed in Santa and the spirit of Christmas, even though other kids his age were telling him differently. Santa asked my Grandpa if he would like to help Santa when he got older."

Tommy couldn't believe it. "You mean Santa Claus asked your grandpa to HELP him? What did Santa want him to do?" asked Tommy excitedly.

Grandpa Jack continued, "Well, it didn't happen right away, and it was several years before he heard from Santa. Grandpa Chuck still always believed in Santa, even when everyone else was telling him there was no Santa Claus."

"One night before Christmas, Grandpa Chuck heard a noise in his living room and went to see what it was. He told me that there, standing in the middle of the room, was Santa Claus, and he was holding a big box wrapped in the most beautiful red and gold paper. Santa told him that now was the time that he wanted him to help."

"Santa came back to see him?" Tommy asked.

"Yes, Tommy," Grandpa Jack said.

"What was in the box?" Tommy excitedly asked. He remembered all the wonderful toys and surprises Santa had given him over the years.

"Tommy, Grandpa Chuck told me that Santa handed him the box and told him to open it very carefully. Grandpa Chuck slowly opened the box and in the box was the most beautiful Santa Claus suit he had ever seen," said Grandpa Jack.

"A Santa Claus suit? What was he supposed to do with a Santa Claus suit, Grandpa?" asked Tommy with a puzzled look on his face.

"Well, here is the good part. Santa told Grandpa Chuck that during the Christmas season, he gets so busy with finishing the toys, checking his lists of good little boys and girls, and people wanting to see him at different parties and events that he needs help. You see, Tommy, Santa doesn't want to disappoint anyone, so he needs people to help him."

"So...Santa, or his main elf, would call Grandpa Chuck when it was impossible for Santa to get to a party or a parade, and Grandpa Chuck would put on that beautiful, magical Santa suit and go to the event. That way, Santa Claus would not disappoint those children and adults that wanted to see him."

"Then Grandpa Chuck did one other thing. When we got home, he told me to follow him. We went into his closet and hanging up was the most beautiful Santa suit I had ever seen. That was the suit that Santa had given him. I couldn't believe my eyes, Tommy. There it was! I don't think I have ever seen anything so beautiful."

"WOW!" said Tommy.

Grandpa Jack went on, "That is the secret, Tommy. Santa has many helpers that look just like him. Only a few get called by Santa to help. They have kept that secret for years."

"You know, Tommy, the spirit of Christmas and Santa Claus are as real as you and me, and it's up to us to keep it alive," said Grandpa Jack.

"Tommy, now you are one of the few that know the secret," said Grandpa Jack.

"Oh, Grandpa, I will keep it to myself," Tommy earnestly vowed.

"Grandpa, do you think that someday I will be able to help Santa Claus?" asked Tommy.

"Tommy, Santa is always looking for people who truly believe in him and the spirit of Christmas. If you truly believe and don't let those other kids bother you, I'm sure Santa will know and maybe someday Santa will show up at your house with a red and gold wrapped present with the most beautiful Santa suit inside," said Grandpa Jack.

"I wish I could have met Great-Great-Grandpa Chuck," said Tommy.

"Well, you would have loved him, especially around Christmas time. Let's go home," and with that Grandpa Jack started the car.

"Ok... and thank you, Grandpa," said Tommy as he leaned back in his seat.

As they drove home Grandpa Jack had a big smile on his face as he listened to Tommy sing, "Here Comes Santa Claus, Here Comes Santa Claus, Right Down Santa Claus Lane!"

When they got to Tommy's house, his mom was waiting at the door. Tommy ran past her and said, "Merrrrry Christmas, Mom!" and ran up to his room.

"Dad, thank you so much, Tommy will remember this always. You know, YOU are a great Santa Claus," she said as she gave him a big hug.

Grandpa Jack threw his head back and laughed a great big laugh, "HO! HO! HO! Well, you know I get it honestly!"

♪♫ HERE COMES SANTA CLAUS,
HERE COMES SANTA CLAUS
HO HO HO ♫♪

Author's Note

I have been a professional Santa Claus for over forty years. One Christmas season, my daughter, her husband and three children were between homes and stayed with my wife, Jane and me. That caused some concern with our grandchildren, Lilly, a fifth-grader, Jack, a second-grader and Bella, eighteen months old. Lilly wanted to believe in Santa but found out the previous year the story behind Santa, Bella was too young, but Jack still believed and was sure to see me, from time to time, dressed up as Santa Claus. So we came up with a story that would hopefully keep Jack believing in Santa and the spirit of Christmas for a few more years. Jack reacted just as "Tommy" did when he was told the story. Hopefully, he will believe in the spirit of Santa Claus and Christmas for many, many years to come, just like his grandfather.

CPSIA information can be obtained
at www.ICGtesting.com
Printed in the USA
LVHW050230301021
701739LV00004B/33